Full Circle

A Parlor Opera

Lyrics by Kristina Burbank

Music by Sheryle Kaluza

Sheryle Kaluza

All rights reserved.
No portion of this book may be reproduced in any
form without the written permission of the publisher.

Copyright 2017

Edgewater Publishing
7958 SW Edgewater
Wilsonville, OR 97070

Table of Contents

Scene One: Goodbye	2
The Chief Decides	3
Sky's Response	6
Mother-Daughter Lament	8
Scene Two: Alive	23
Journey Duet (Recitative)	24
Journey Duet	31
Scene Three: Journey	36
Struggle Duet	37
Scene Four: Home	44
If Only for Today	46
Where is She Tonight?	54
Scene Five: Dreams	66
Grandmother Moon	67
Willow's Nightmare	73
O, Morning	80
Scene Six: Forgiven	86
Reunion Trio	87
If Only	105
Nessu and Annali Reunion	115
Return to the River	118
Scene Seven: Full Circle	126
One People Again	127
Acknowledgements	132

Characters

Old man/narrator: He is elderly and knows the stories of his people by heart. He is Nessu's descendent, many generations removed.

Annali (Ahn-ah-lee): [means Mother] She is 75 and was a skilled seamstress. She is stiff with arthritis and mobility is difficult for her. She gave birth to Willow late in life and her husband, much her senior, died long ago.

Sky: She is 65 and never married. Despite a withered right hand and a stiff left ankle, she was a skilled hunter in her youth.

Willow: She is 40. A skilled tanner, she leaves her best flint knife and a skein of leather lacings with her mother, thereby insuring her survival. Her husband died in a hunting accident when her son was an infant.

Nessu (Nay-soo): [means Homecoming] He is a young teen. His prized possession is an eagle feather found near a summer campsite. He leaves it with his grandmother as a sign of hope. When he is young, people call him Feather. Later in life they will call him Chief.

The Chief: He is middle aged and has successfully led the tribe for many years. But now the ways he's always trusted seem to be failing.   On the darkest of nights, he stands alone in deep shadows praying for morning—yearning for some new path to travel.

Narrator's Preamble:

You have asked for a story and I will tell you one, one my mother told me. One as old as time. As old as humankind. The strong ones take what the weak ones have. Maybe their food. Maybe their robes. Maybe even their lives.

And they think no one will ever know.

But the wind knows. She sweeps over all the earth tasting the sweetness of love and the bitterness of death, and nothing is hidden from her. Late at night from the place of dreams she whispers to those strong ones, "What have you done? What have you done?"

You may ask yourself, "Will the story ever change?"

Maybe if the strong become weak, you think, there can be a new beginning.

Maybe if the weak become strong, they will remember the pain of weakness and be kind. Maybe they will be caring and generous and that will change things.

You can be sure the wind will ask them all. Late at night from the place of dreams she will whisper, "What will you do? Who will you be?"

Long ago all people walked together. But their path became bruised and crooked. And even though it led straight to a dangerous precipice, and each of them knew they would fall, no one would turn aside. No one would circle back for a new beginning.

My mother told me that life will come full circle only when the strong and the weak walk together again. Then sleep will come easy and dreams will be deep. Then life, even when it is hard, will be good.

When the wind whispers to you, may you have the courage of the young and the wisdom of the old when you answer. "What will you do? Who will you be?"

But I digress. Here is the story I promised you.

SCENE ONE: Goodbye

Old Man:

One cold winter in a time long ago and in a place far away my ancestors were starving. The great lake where they camped was frozen solid. Wind howled and snow drifted against their tents and clung in thick clumps to evergreen boughs. Birch trees stood like a forest of skeletons providing plenty of wood for the fires, but nothing to put in the pots.

To make matters worse, a whole flock of ravens now lay dead in the snow. Most of the birds had fallen near the camp of the two slow ones—Sky and Annali—who had pitched their tent away from the others and closer to their trapping lines. Soon children, already weak and hungry, began running fevers and shaking with chills. Several even died.

So, the elders approached their chief. "This is a bad omen," they said. "Look what these slow ones have brought upon us. They've always held us back and eaten food needed by our hunters. And now this!" "We must move," said the elders. "And we must leave the slow ones behind."

Their solution was not a new one. For generations, in times of starvation and crisis, the strong had left the weak behind. It was not a kind way, but it the only way they knew to survive. And it was the way things had always been.

The Chief reminded himself of all these things as he prepared to speak. Still it troubled him as it always had. He set his face in a stoic mask and called all the people together.

Then in his fullest, deepest voice, he made his announcement and walked away. For a moment, no one else moved, each frozen in stunned silence. Sky stood to confront those who remained, but Annali sank deep within herself remembering an old lullaby she once sang to Willow, her daughter.

"Who will speak up for us?" Sky cried out. But the tribe maintained an ominous silence, and began to pack and then leave. Only Willow and her son, Nessu, hung back to say goodbye. But then, having left parting gifts--Nessu, an eagle feather, and Willow, her best flint knife and skein of leather lacings--they too deserted the slow ones."

As they left, Annali's words cut her daughter to the bone.

Music: Chief's Announcement
Sky's Response
Mother-Daughter Lament

The Chief Decides
Chief

Burbank
Kaluza

© 2017 Sheryle Kaluza and Kristina Burbank

The Chief Decides page 2

We must leave the slow ones here a-lone. mmm. Strike the tents, load the sleds. We will leave be-fore the ris-ing of the sun. mmm.

wolves howling

We are like wild an-i-mals, leav-ing our old and our lame.

Sky's Response

Sky

Burbank   Kaluza

© 2017 Sheryle Kaluza and Kristina Burbank

Mother Daughter Lament
Willow, Annali

Kaluza

© 2017 Sheryle Kaluza and Kristina Burbank

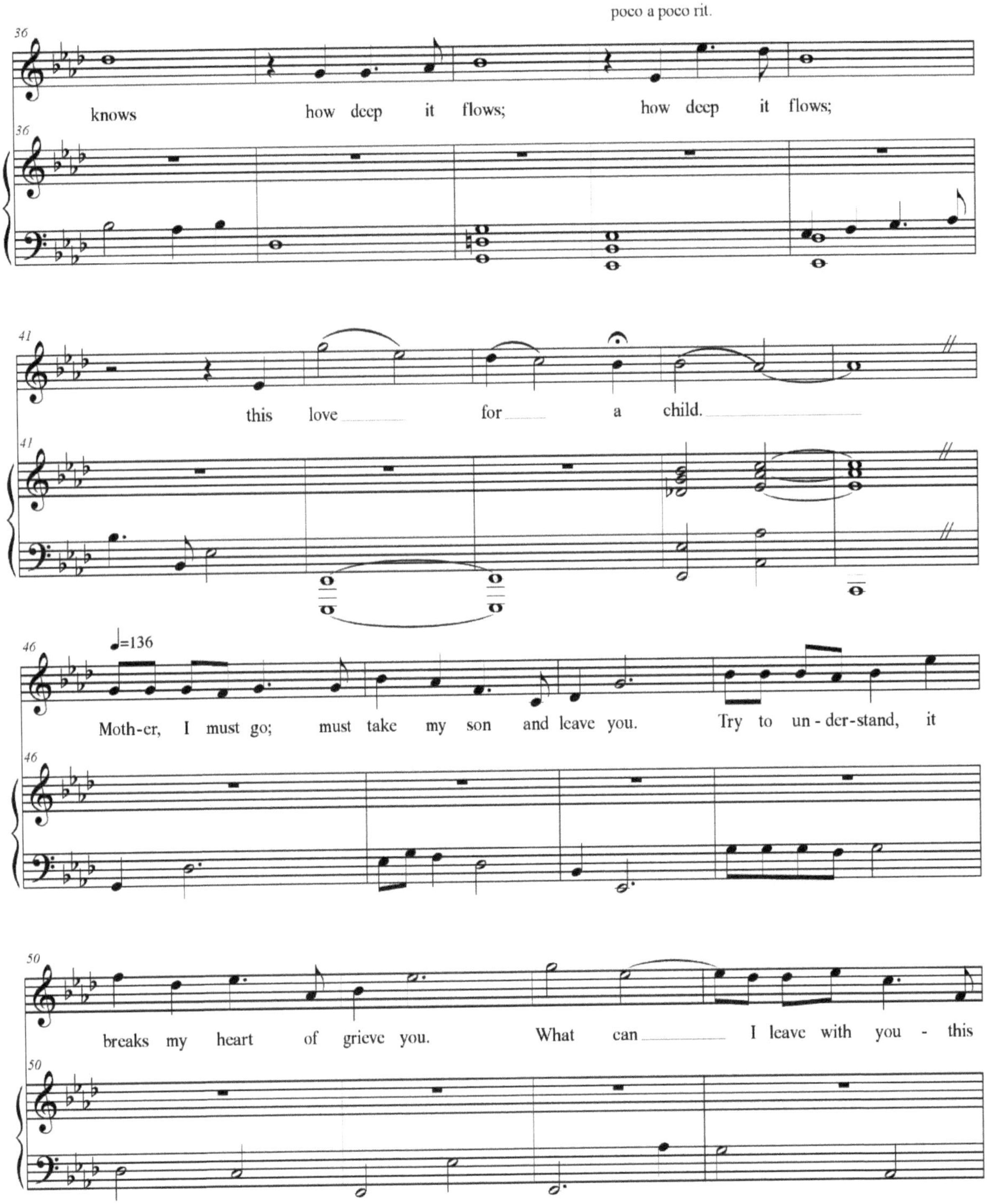

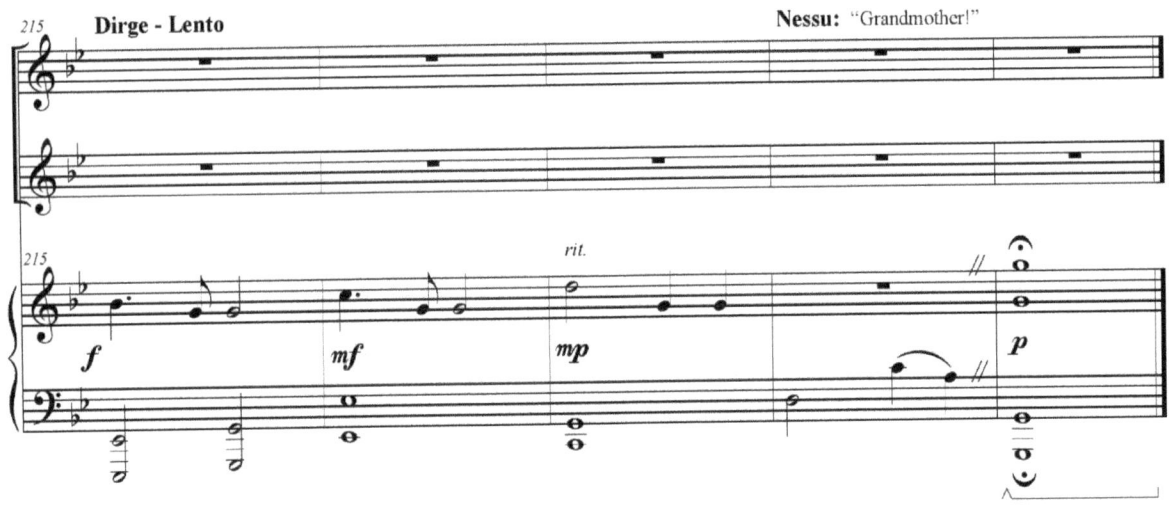

SCENE TWO: Alive

Old Man:
    That first night was very hard for the two women. Wolves howled and bad dreams troubled their sleep. They awoke with a sense of despair and utter isolation. For a long while, they simply stared at one another. Finally, they spoke, taking stock of their situation. They had a tent. They had fire and wood. They had a few scraps of dried fish and berries. They had a knife and lacings. They could make traps and snowshoes. They could make wooden spears—sharpening and hardening tips in the fire.
    And they took stock of themselves. They were both slow and neither of them was young. But they were wise and they were skilled. And they were alive.
    Realizing they must leave the sickness that surrounded them, they made plans to head northwest, even deeper into the heart of winter, seeking an old campground abandoned long ago.
    Giving themselves very little time to grieve, they turned to the work at hand. Sky insisted on incinerating the dead ravens, watching as the smoke turned from black to silver white against the frozen sky. She'd always loved ravens for their brightness and humor and even now she dreamed of flying with them.

*   Music: [Annali and Sky] Journey Recitative*
*   Journey Duet*

Journey Duet (Recitative)
Annali, Sky

Burbank　　　　　　　　　　　　　　　　　　　　　　　　　　　　　　Kaluza

© 2017 Sheryle Kaluza and Kristina Burbank

Journey Duet

Annali, Sky

Burbank

Kaluza

© 2017 Sheryle Kaluza and Kristina Burbank

Journey Duet page 5

35

SCENE THREE: Journey

Old Man:
    The two women spent the better part of a week preparing for their journey to the ancient summer fishing grounds. Then, early one morning, they broke camp, carefully loading and balancing their sleds. Annali tucked Nessu's eagle feather deep into the folds of her shirt as she took her first few steps.
    They struggled on day after day, mile after mile, sometimes singing to keep their spirits alive. Sky led slowly and steadily, her left snowshoe dragging slightly, her spear tucked under her right arm, while Annali followed a few yards behind.
    Pulling the sleds tied to their waists, they used their inverted spears as walking sticks to steady themselves and to test the depth of the snow as they advanced.
    Each evening they made camp, melting snow to prepare a weak fish broth and a tea made of spruce buds to fill their aching stomachs. Then they ate a few dried berries, chewing them long and well as if they were the richest of foods.
    Early in the morning of the day that proved to be the last of their journey, Sky was awakened by the raspy cawing of a raven. Throughout the day, it urged them along, finally leading them home.

Music: [Annali and Sky] Struggle Duet

Struggle Duet

Annali, Sky

Burbank

Kaluza

Struggle Duet page 7

SCENE FOUR: Home

Old Man:

After their long journey, the two set up camp in a willow grove, pitching a tent, building a fire and resting for the night. In the morning, they began rebuilding their lives.

Through that long winter they hunted and trapped and built their drying racks—dreaming of fat salmon and trout. Then through the warm spring and summer they gathered great caches of dried fish, meat and furs. They fell into familiar roles—one hunting, the other minding the fire and sewing. And their years fell away like dried leaves. They were not young but they were alive and prospering.

Then one late autumn day, after weeks of working closely together, Sky and Annali spent a long day apart. While Annali minded the camp, sewing and cooking, Sky went out to gather nuts and berries, taking her spear with her for protection.

As Sky harvested hackberries, she spotted the tracks of a single large caribou. Setting out in the slow, loping, albeit stiff gait of a hunter, she began to track him. Hours passed as she followed, occasionally glimpsing a patch of hide or part of an antler through the underbrush.

Finally, an old bull, his muzzle white with age, revealed himself across a small meadow. He stood quietly watching her, his posture alert, the cold air humming with his vitality and steaming with his breath. Sky braced herself and prepared to launch her spear, but stopped without releasing it.

She realized that even if her aim were true, she would only have wounded him. And having no desire to do unnecessary harm, she dropped her spear to her side and watched him as he tossed his head and slipped into the woods.

Suddenly exhausted, Sky paused to catch her breath.

Music: [Sky Hunting Aria] If Only for Today

If Only for Today
Sky

Burbank · Kaluza

© 2017 Sheryle Kaluza and Kristina Burbank

If Only for Today   page 7

Old Man:

    Like her name, Sky reflected light. But for Annali, steeped in the bitterness of abandonment, darkness was never far away. She loved her daughter, but looked down on her too.

    Often a great loneliness would encompass her, at times so deep that she felt it would destroy her. But other times this same loneliness was strangely healing. Like a great poultice it drew out her bitterness and grief, casting them into the vast darkness between the stars. Strangely enough, loneliness eventually became her dearest friend.

Music: [Annali Sewing Aria] Where Is She Tonight?

Where is She Tonight?
Annali, Willow

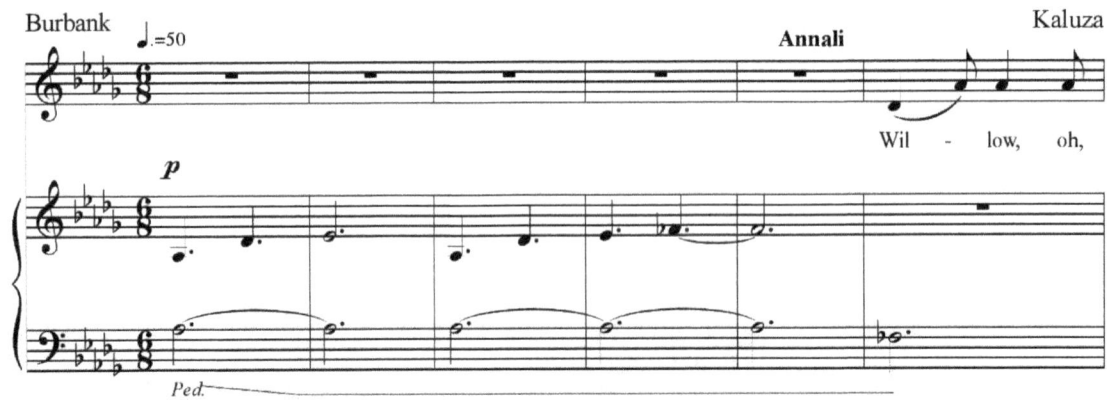

© 2017 Sheryle Kaluza & Kristina Burbank

Where is She Tonight? page 2

55

SCENE FIVE: Dreams

Old Man:
    Just then, Sky stumbled into camp. "Where have you been?" cried Annali. "How you have worried me!"
    "I hunted a caribou all day, but came home with berries." Sky mimed her hunt, crouching, jogging a few stiff steps, hand pressed to her back. Her humor melted Annali's anger. They ate and talked, grateful for each other and for a hot meal. Then they sat down back-to-back as was their custom before sleep, for it was good to feel the warmth and breathing of a friend.
    But each of them realized how fragile their circle of warmth and light was and how immeasurably deep and cold was the unforgiving land around them. As they fell into the arms of sleep, dreams of old friends and family embraced them as winter cast its icy shadow over them.
    Soon the two women fell asleep with full bellies, surrounded by plenty. But many miles away at the tribe's campground every detail spoke of poverty, hunger and despair. The Chief huddled at his own scant fire, while Nessu and his mother huddled at theirs. Each was restless with dreams.
    But only Nessu's dreams were sweet. For as time had passed, he'd grown increasingly confident that his grandmother survived, and more convinced than ever that he must find her. The Chief and people might stay with the old ways, he told himself, but he would find a new way.

Music: [Nessu Aria] Grandmother Moon

Grandmother Moon

Nessu

Burbank Kaluza

© 2017 Sheryle Kaluza and Kristina Burbank

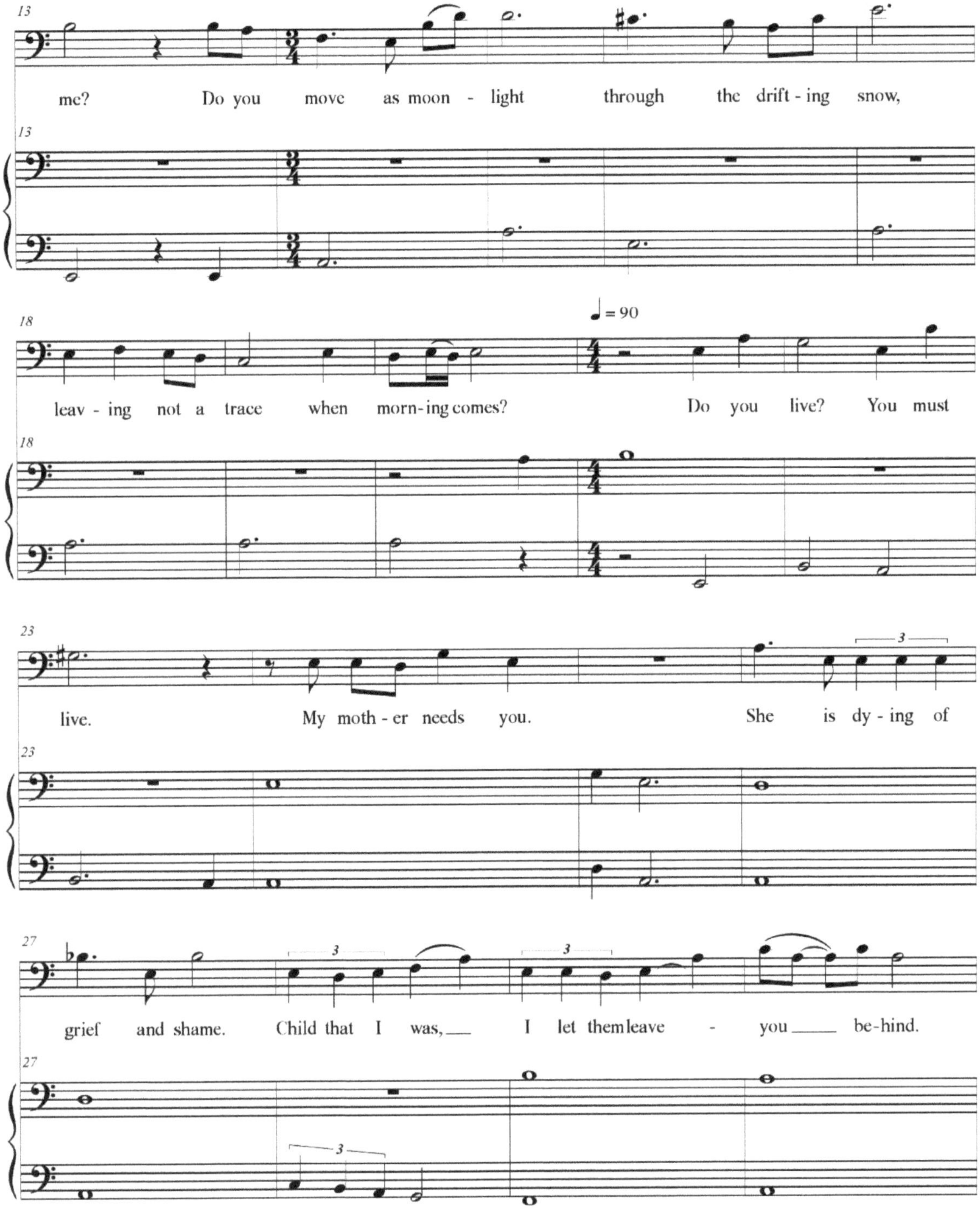

Old Man:
Impulsively, Nessu made ready to leave the camp in search of his grandmother. He quickly picked up his spear and gathered his few belongings into a bundle. But just as he turned to leave, he was interrupted by his mother's nightmare.

Willow had bolted from her bed. Half-standing, draped in her bedding, she stared wild-eyed into the darkness beyond her campfire. Believing that she saw wolves attacking her mother, she cried out a fearful warning.

Music: [Willow and Nessu Recitative and Aria] Willow's Nightmare

Willow's Nightmare

Willow, Nessu

Burbank

Kaluza

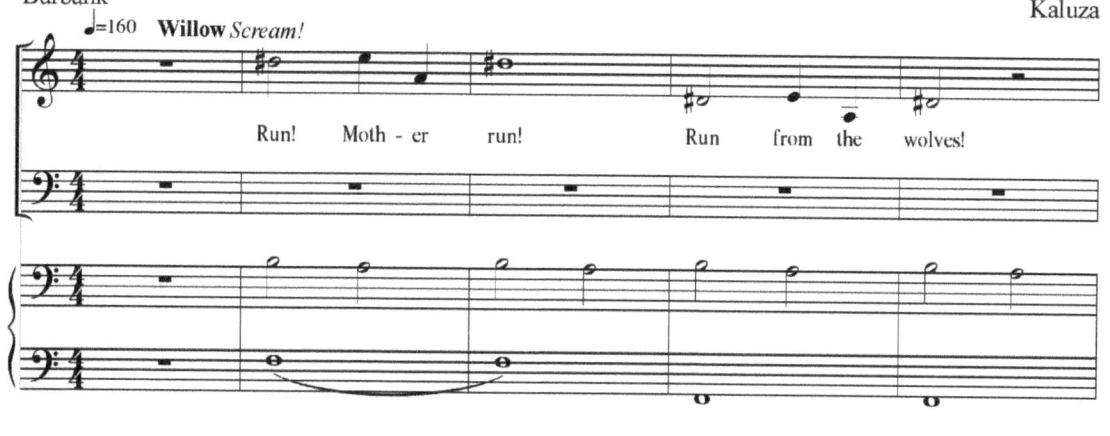

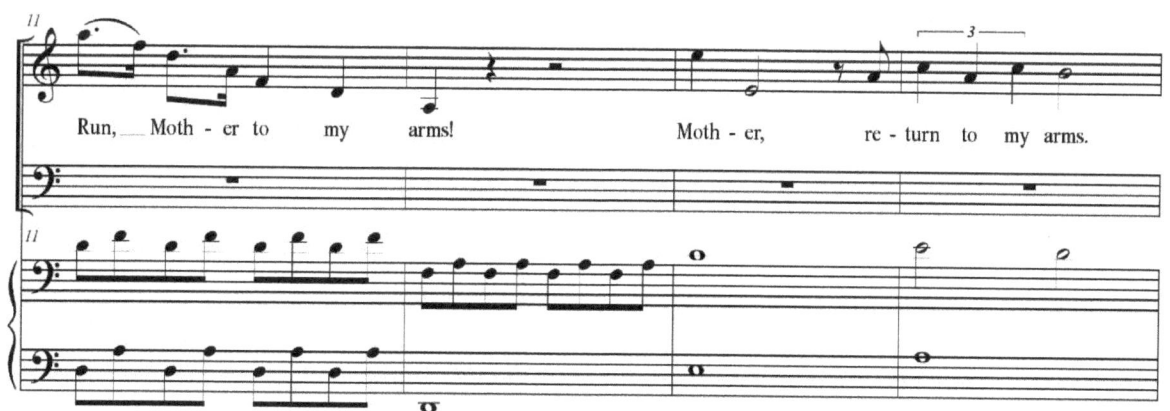

© 2017 Sheryle Kaluza and Kristina Burbank

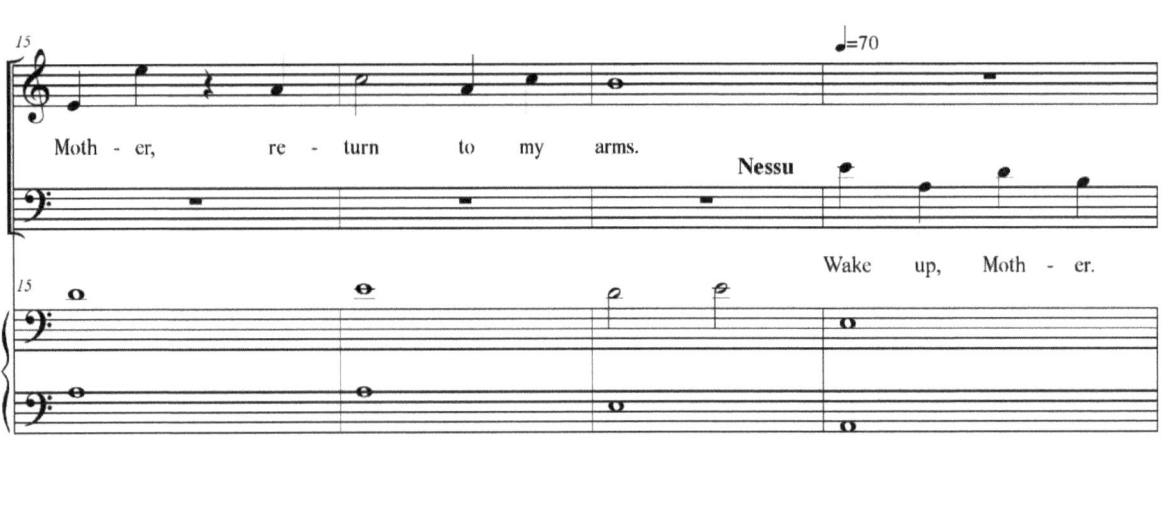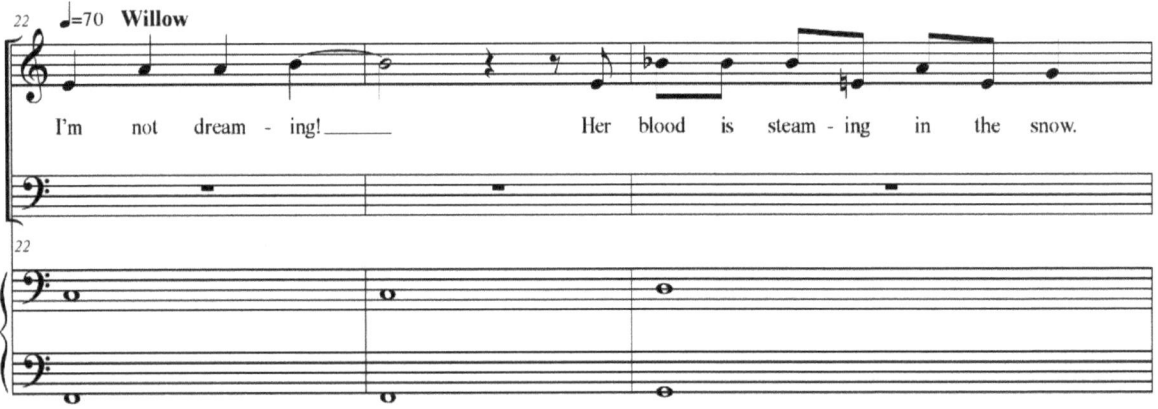

Old Man:

When his mother finally slept, Nessu picked up his spear and bundle and turned to go, but found the Chief blocking his way. They struggled briefly, but the older, stronger man soon subdued the younger, forcing him to drop his gear. Once he was subdued, the chief released him saying: "How brave you are, Nessu, and how foolish. If you die searching for your grandmother, and if your mother dies of grief, who will be left? What will be gained?

Nessu snapped back "What will we gain waiting here? We will all starve!"

The Chief was stunned at his impertinence. "Hold your tongue, Nessu. Wait here with your Mother, in the morning I'll send scouts. Soon enough we will know for sure if they've survived."

Music: [Chief Aria] O, Morning

O, Morning
Chief

Burbank   Kaluza

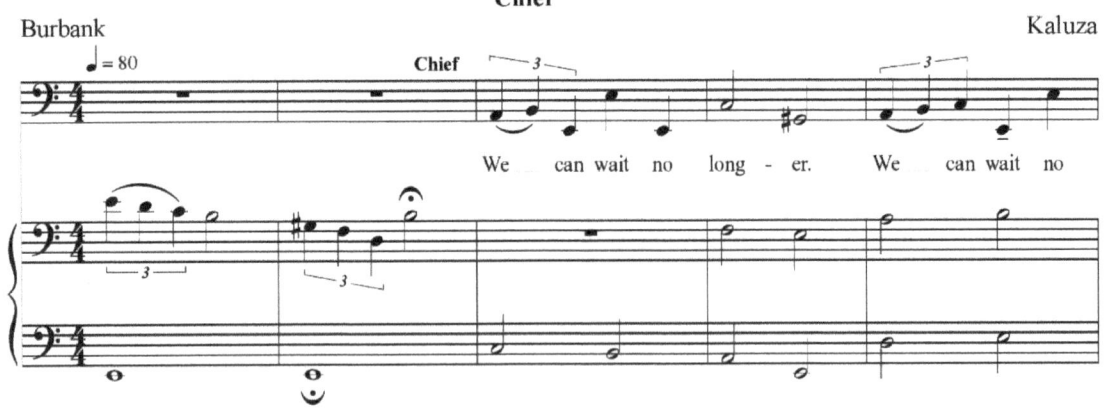

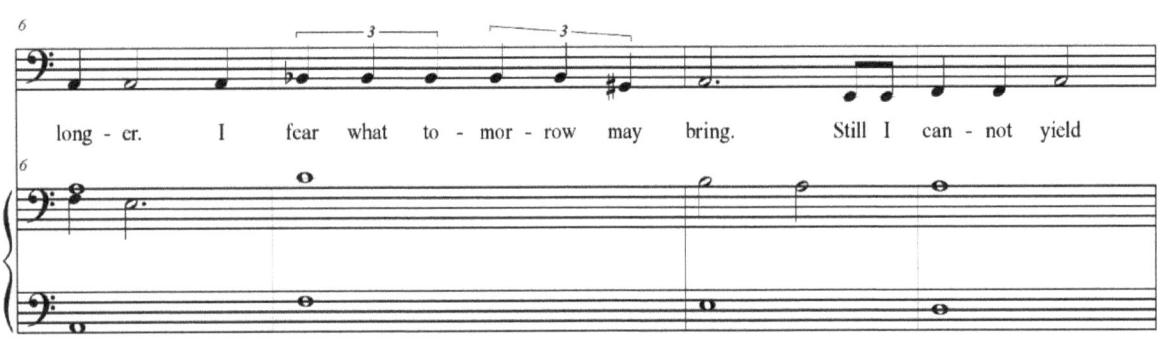

© 2017 Sheryle Kaluza and Kristina Burbank

SCENE SIX: Forgiven

Old Man:

In the morning, it was the Chief himself who went searching for the two women. You may ask yourself, "Why did he go alone?" A man like the Chief could say to another man, "Go here and do this", and he would. And it's true that he could have sent a lesser man. But as he looked around that morning, the Chief did not see a lesser man. So, he went himself.

It was a new way to do things. Was he brave or foolish? Was he right or wrong? He could not possibly know until the thing was done.

As he jogged over miles of frozen terrain, he wondered what he would say if he found the two women. Could he demand they return? After all it would be weak to plead. And chiefs don't plead.

Still he realized he had been wrong. Should he admit it? Could he admit it? After all, the tribe was only as strong as its leader. And any sign of weakness would vibrate through the whole community like cracks in river ice.

He knew how Annali would respond to any show of weakness – unyielding and angry. But Sky might be more understanding. For though she was strong, her strength was tempered by her own lameness. She was the one person he knew who could perceive both strength and weakness in another – and still recognize wholeness.

The Chief pushed on for several days, resting only briefly each night. When he arrived at the camp site at the great lake, he found it completely abandoned. That night as sleep eluded him, he wondered where the two might have gone. If they were running, he reasoned, they would go south. If they were hiding, they might go north. Who would want to follow them there?

When at last he slept he dreamed of himself as a young boy, standing on a sunny river bank trying to spear a great fish with a slender green willow stick. On the opposite bank two older girls were pulling in a net filled with shimmering salmon.

When he awoke he knew where the two slow ones had gone--to the ancient summer fishing grounds in the far north. They were like spawning salmon returning to ancient waters born in the stone-cold mountains far beyond the farthest horizon. Strapping on his pack and notching up his resolve, he headed north at the break of day.

One morning a few days later, when his meager rations were gone and his energy was completely depleted, two ravens, hopping and cawing, led him to a recent wolf kill. There he harvested enough marrow and shreds of meat to survive the final leg of his journey. That day he rested and ate.

Then he traveled again and two days later, just before dawn, he saw a flicker of light from a campfire hidden in a willow grove. He called out, "Sky! Annali!"

"We're here," they replied. Admitting their fear only to one another, they stood tall and proud waiting for him at their campfire. When he arrived, there was a long silence before the Chief lowered his eyes and spoke.

Music: [Annali, Sky and Chief] Reunion Trio
[Chief and Sky Duet] If Only

Reunion Trio
Sky, Annali, Chief

Reunion Trio 13

If Only
Sky, Chief

Burbank — ♩= 50

Kaluza

Chief

If only I were strong and sure a-gain. If time were new and life would move a-gain. If only I were half the man I was. If only we could all be-gin a-gain. If on-ly, If on-ly I were young and

© 2017 Sheryle Kaluza and Kristina Burbank

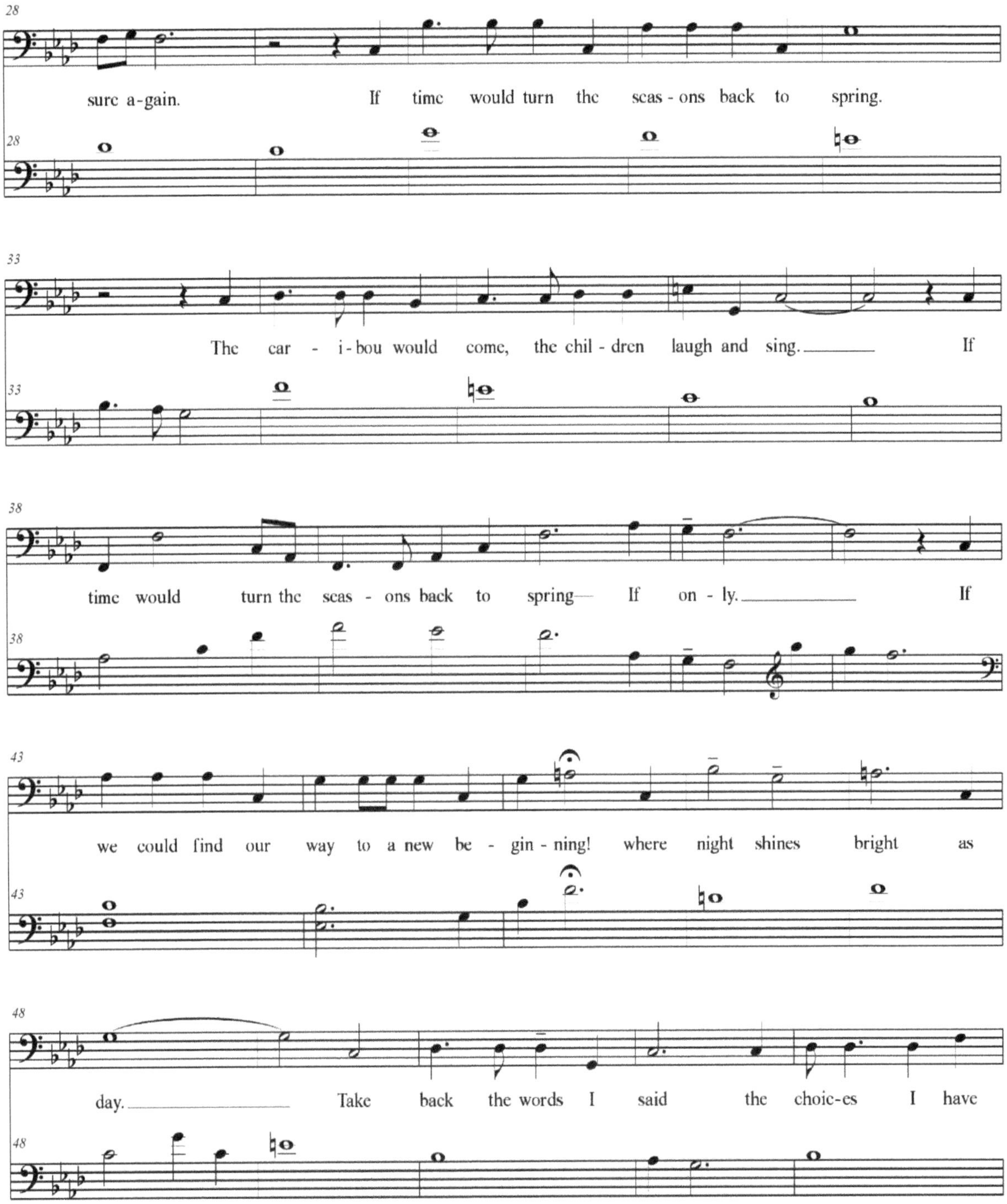

If Only   page 4

But if we walk to-geth - er, we will come full cir - cle. We will be one peo-ple a - gain. If on - ly. If on - ly. If on - ly I were young and sure a - gain. There's

If Only page 5

109

If Only page 7

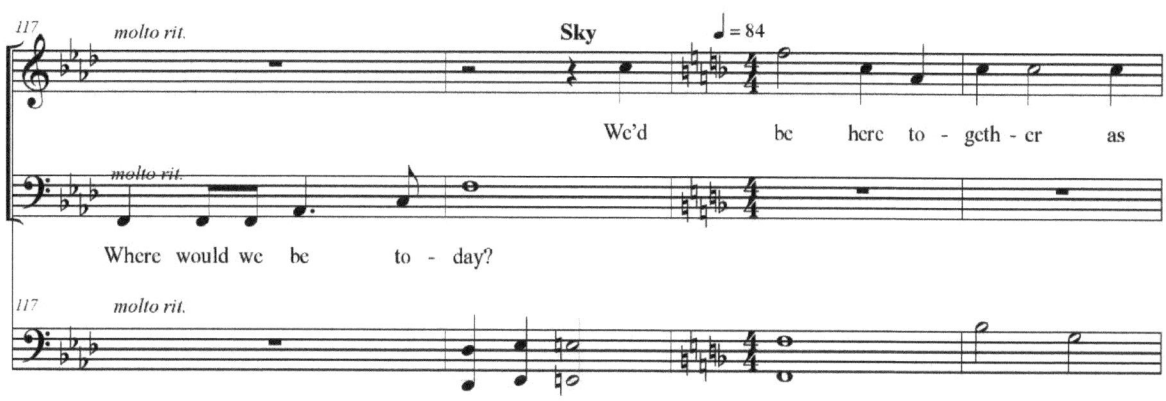
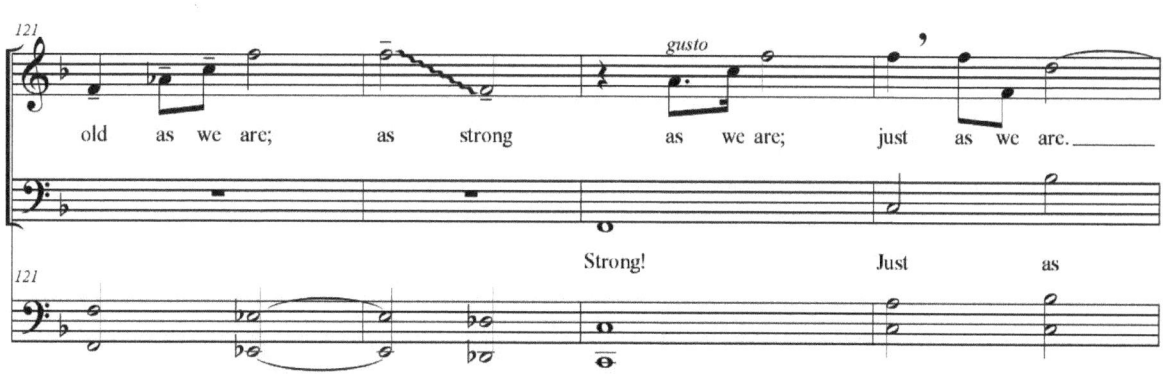
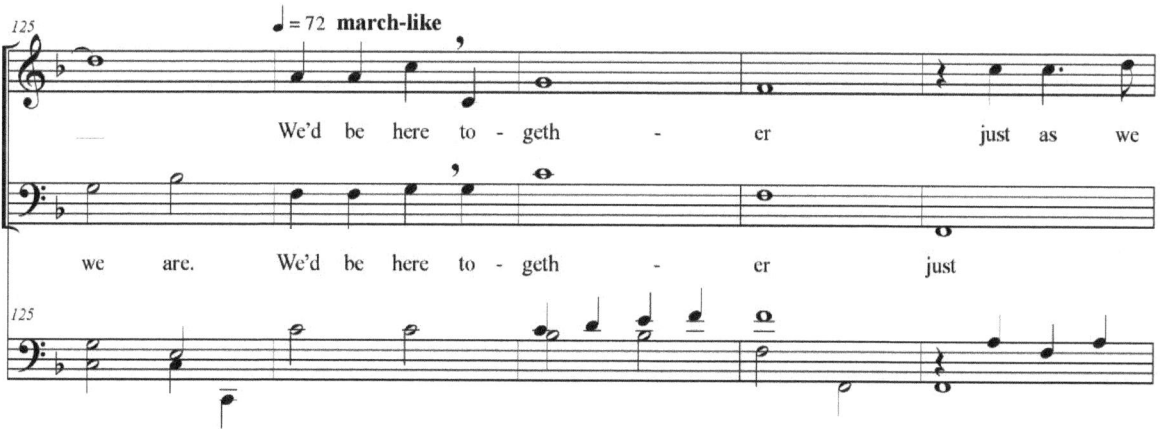

Old Man:
    Though the Chief hadn't realized it, Nessu and his mother had been following him. For the night after he'd left, Willow had dreamed that the moon would lead them to Annali. Unable to wait for the Chief's return, she and her son had set out on their own. During the night, they followed the moon and during the day, they followed a lone raven who faithfully flew ahead.
    The day the Chief had rested, Willow and her son had closed the distance between them. And for the last few miles of their journey, he'd left a trail of frosty footsteps for them to follow.
    When they finally neared the camp of the two women, Nessu raced ahead, as Willow followed a short distance behind. As he drew near, he cried out three times, "Grandmother!"
    Hearing him, Annali turned toward him, dropping a large basket of goods, standing empty-handed, calling out his name as he rushed to her. They fell into one another's arms, laughing until they cried. Placing her hands first on his face, then on his shoulders, she cried, "How I have missed you!" Then, taking the eagle feather from her shirt, she wove it into his hair.
    Annali said, "How tall and thin you've grown! How hungry you must be!" She led him to a place by the fire, giving him fish and broth, while Willow watched silently from the shadows of the nearby trees.
    "Where is your mother, Nessu?" Annali asked.
    "Nearby," he replied.
    "When will she come to me?"
    "Only when you call for her, Grandmother. She thinks you hate her."
    "O Nessu, I love her! Tell her I love her." Willow then stepped out of the shadows. Mother and daughter drew together in a long, wordless and healing embrace.

Music:
    [Duet Nessu and Annali] Nessu and Annali Reunion
    [Duet Annali and Willow] Return to the River

Nessu and Annali Reunion
Nessu, Annali

Burbank / Kaluza

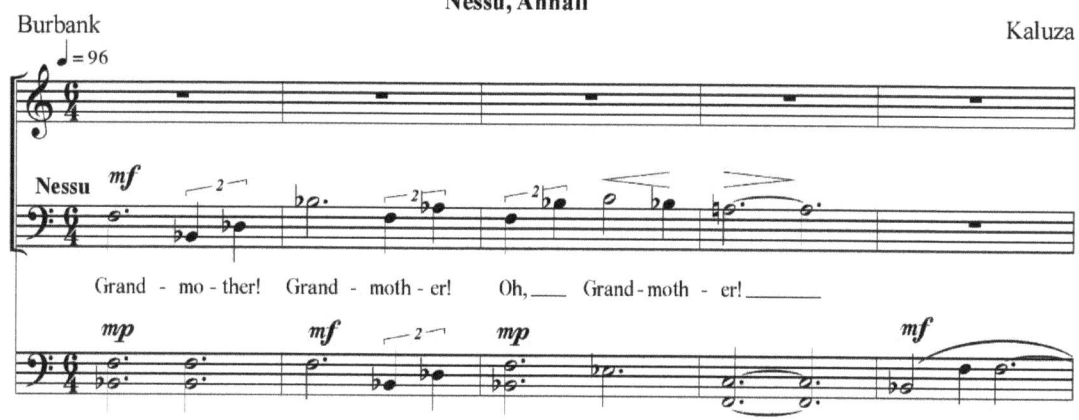

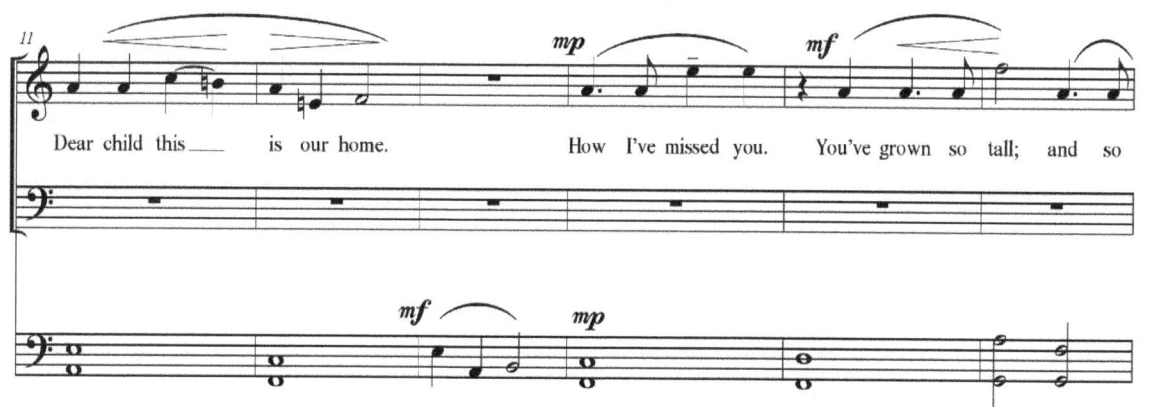

© 2017 Sheryle Kaluza and Kristina Burbank

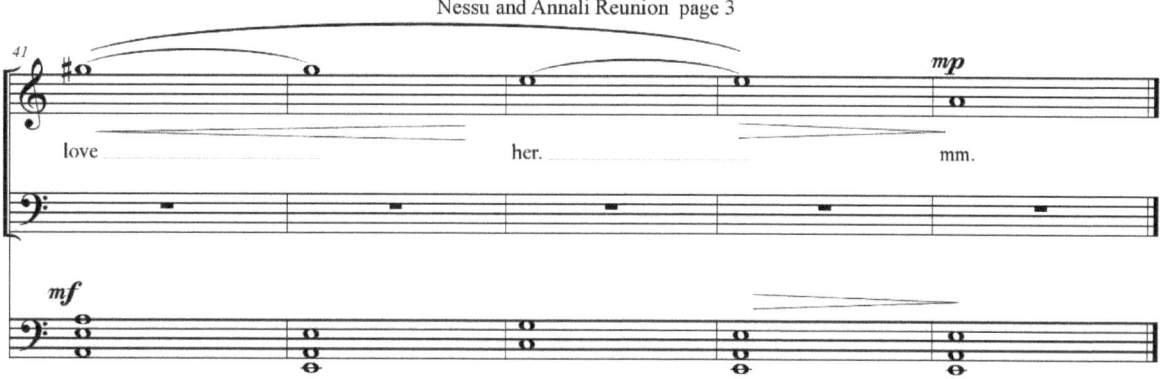

Return to the River

Willow, Annali

Burbank

Kaluza

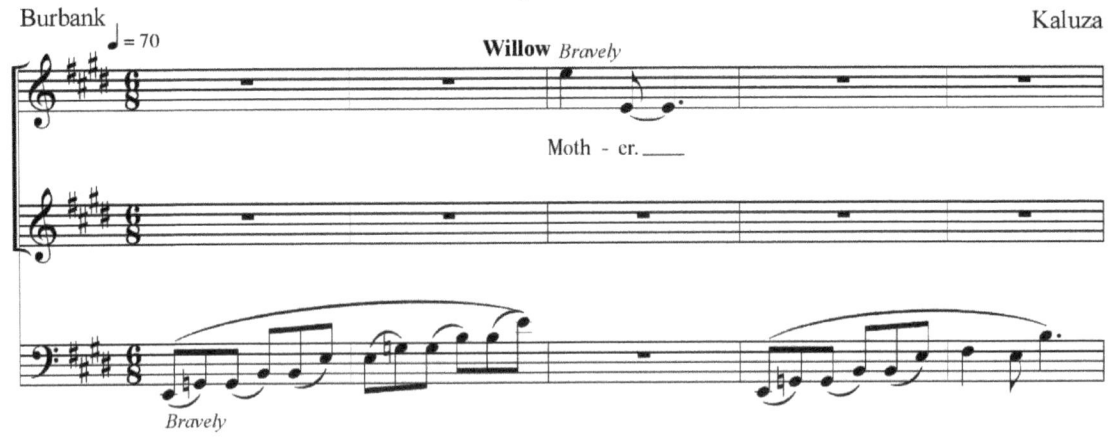

© 2017 Sheryle Kaluza and Kristina Burbank

Return to the River page 2

SCENE SEVEN: Full Circle

Old Man:
That night the five of them gathered around a single campfire. A flock of ravens, heads tucked under their wings, their work done, roosted in the boughs above them.

The people ate and talked a little about old times and old friends. They talked about the future they would share together. Still, they talked as if they had become a little like strangers to one another. They were like dancers who stumble remembering old steps.

Maybe because it was still hard to speak about themselves, people talked about the moon which shown so brightly that night. Maybe it felt more secure to hang their hopes on something higher than each other. But later, when Nessu led them in a slow circle dance, it felt good to lean on one another too.

Finally, when the dance was over, and the fire had burned down to embers, they arranged themselves for sleep. Tired bones and muscles gave up their burdens, sinking deeply into the comfort of new bedding. The howling of a wolf faded far into the distance.

Then as their breathing settled into the rhythm of the night, sleep came easy, and dreams were deep. And when they awoke the next morning, and in the days to come, they found that life, though hard, was good.

Music: [Full Ensemble] One People Again

One People Again
Chief, Annali, Nessu, Sky, Willow

Burbank — Kaluza

©2017 Sheryle Kaluza and Kristina Burbank

The authors would like to thank the many people who provided encouragement and help with this endeavor.

Music Notation…Linda Missad

Cover Design…Tatiana Villa

Caribou Artist…Nora Sherwood

Document Format…Charles Kaluza

Narrative Edit…Ron Lovell

General Artwork…Contributing Artists at Shutterstock

Original Notation help…Joelle Schaal

Sheryle would especially like to thank her parents for trading their 30-cup coffee maker for a piano when she was 8 years old.